For my great aunt Sylvia Bond

Copyright © 1991 by Stephen Butler
First published in Great Britain
by Frances Lincoln Limited.

Library of Congress Cataloging in Publication Data
Butler, Stephen, 1962– Henny Penny / by Stephen Butler.   p.   cm.
SUMMARY: Henny Penny and her friends are
on their way to tell the king that the sky
is falling when they meet a hungry fox.
ISBN 0-688-09921-1 — ISBN 0-688-09922-X (lib. bdg.)
[1. Folklore.]   I. Title.
PZ8.1.B96He   1991   398.24′528617—dc20
[E] 90-35115   CIP   AC

Printed in Hong Kong
First U.S. edition
1   3   5   7   9   10   8   6   4   2

HENNY PENNY

STEPHEN BUTLER

Tambourine Books · New York

One day while Henny Penny was sitting beneath
the oak tree an acorn fell and hit her on the head.
"Goodness me! The sky is falling!" she cried.
"I must go and tell the king."

So Henny Penny ran off in a great hurry to tell the king the sky was falling.
She had not gone far before she met…

Cocky Locky.
"Where are you going, Henny Penny?" asked Cocky Locky.
"Oh, Cocky Locky! The sky is falling!" cried Henny Penny.
"And I am going to tell the king."
"Goodness me!" said Cocky Locky. "I'll come with you."

So Henny Penny and Cocky Locky hurried on to tell
the king the sky was falling.
They had not gone far before they met…

Ducky Lucky.
"Where are you two going?" asked Ducky Lucky.
"Oh, Ducky Lucky! The sky is falling!" cried Henny Penny.
"And we are going to tell the king."
"Goodness me!" said Ducky Lucky. "I'll come with you."

So Henny Penny, Cocky Locky, and Ducky Lucky
hurried on to tell the king the sky was falling.
They had not gone far before they met...

Goosey Loosey.

"Where are you all going?" asked Goosey Loosey.

"Oh, Goosey Loosey! The sky is falling!" cried
Henny Penny. "And we are going to tell the king."

"Goodness me!" said Goosey Loosey. "I'll come with you."

So Henny Penny, Cocky Locky, Ducky Lucky, and
Goosey Loosey hurried on to tell the king the sky
was falling.
They had not gone far before they met…

Turkey Lurkey.

"Where are you all going?" asked Turkey Lurkey.

"Oh, Turkey Lurkey! The sky is falling!" cried
Henny Penny. "And we are going to tell the king."

"Goodness me!" said Turkey Lurkey. "I'll come with you."

So Henny Penny, Cocky Locky, Ducky Lucky,
Goosey Loosey, and Turkey Lurkey hurried on
to tell the king the sky was falling.

Suddenly Foxy Loxy appeared.
"And where are you all going in such a hurry?" he asked.
"Oh, Foxy Loxy! The sky is falling!" cried Henny Penny.
"We are going to tell the king."

"But you're going the wrong way!" said Foxy Loxy.
"The king's palace is *that* way."
And he pointed to a path leading into the woods.

So Henny Penny, Cocky Locky, Ducky Lucky, Goosey Loosey, and Turkey Lurkey hurried down the path. They ran on and on...until at last they reached the king's palace.

"Come in and tell me your story, Henny Penny," said the king.

But as Henny Penny curtsied, she saw a bushy red tail beneath the king's robe.
"It's a trap!" she cried. "Run!"

Foxy Loxy threw off his cunning disguise
and sprang to the door.

"Surprise!" laughed Foxy Loxy, licking his lips.
"I'm going to eat you all for dinner...."

Henny Penny woke up with a start and opened her eyes. She was still trembling. "Goodness me!" she yawned. "I must have been dreaming."

But just then an acorn fell and hit her on the head.
"Goodness me! The sky is falling!" she cried.
"I must go and tell the king...."

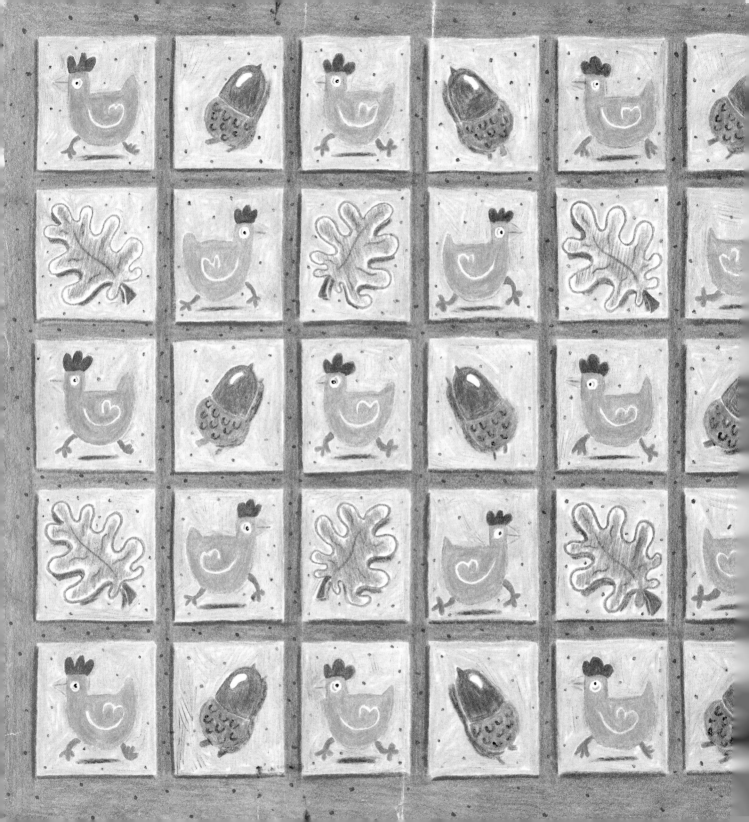